This edition published by Parragon Books Ltd in 2014 and distributed by

Parragon Inc.
440 Park Avenue South, 13th Floor
New York, NY 10016
www.parragon.com

ISBN 978-1-4723-7842-2

Printed in China

Ariel's

Book of Secrets

Parragon

Bath • New York • Cologne • Melbourne • Delhi
Hong Kong • Shenzhen • Singapore • Amsterdam

This book belongs to

Contents

All about you

Ariel wants to know all about you, especially your best secrets! Write them down on these pages.

Name: ....

Nickname: ....

Hair color: ....

Eye color: ....

Birthday: ....

Age: ....

Lucky number: ....

Best friends: ....

....

....

....

Favorite animal: ....

Favorite color: ....

Favorite season: ....

Favorite flower: ....

My best talent: ....

My worst habit: ....

The thing I'm most proud of: ....

....

....

....

My happiest moment: ....

....

....

....

Pretty pictures

Have an adult help you stick photos onto these pages. Ariel has included pictures of her best friends and Prince Eric.

Me as a baby

My best friend

Prince Eric

Flounder & Sebastian

Me on vacation

My favorite thing

My family

Sweet secrets

All your secrets are safe with Ariel!

My biggest secret:

....

....

....

....

....

My secret wish for this year:

....

....

....

....

....

....

A secret I want to tell somebody:

....

....

....

....

A secret I have already shared:

....

....

....

....

My secret dream for when I grow up:

....

....

....

....

Loyal friends

Ariel's friends are very important to her. Sebastian and Flounder are always there when she needs them. Who are your best friends? Write about them on these pages.

Name: ....

Hair color: ....

Eye color: ....

Their best talent: ....

....

What I like about them: ....

....

Name: ....

Hair color: ....

Eye color: ....

Their best talent: ....

....

What I like about them: ....

....

Name: ....

Hair color: ....

Eye color: ....

Their best talent: ....

....

What I like about them: ....

....

....

....

Friendship photographs

Fill these pages with your favorite photographs of your friends!

Bubbly birthdays

Fill in your friends' and relatives' birthdays on these pages.
Think about what you might give them as a gift.
Ariel likes to make seashell necklaces for her friends.

Name: ....

Birthday: ....

Age this year: ....

Gift ideas: ....

....

Name: ....

Birthday: ....

Age this year: ....

Gift ideas: ....

....

....

....

Name: ....

Birthday: ....

Age this year: ....

Gift ideas: ....

....

Name: ....

Birthday: ....

Age this year: ....

Gift ideas: ....

....

Name: ....

Birthday: ....

Age this year: ....

Gift ideas: ....

....

Underwater party

Ariel loves to throw parties for her friends and Prince Eric.
Use these pages to plan your own princess party!
Ariel has added some of her own ideas to help you.

Guest list:

....

....

....

....

....

....

....

....

Party food and drinks:

Shell-shaped candy

Party music:

What games will you play?

Pin the tail on the mermaid

My family

Ariel's father is King Triton, and she likes to visit him under the sea whenever she can. What is your family like? Write about it on these pages.

Who is the funniest? ....

Who makes the most mess? ....

Who is good at helping out? ....

Who takes care of everyone? ....

....

How would your family describe you?

....

....

....

....

....

....

Stick your favorite family photograph here!

Animal friends

Ariel loves sea creatures, and counts them as her friends. Do you have any animal friends? If you don't have a pet, fill in these pages for your dream pet.

Type of animal: ....

Name: ....

Age: ....

Fur or body color: ....

Eye color: ....

Best trick: ....

Favorite food:...

The thing I like best about them: ....

....

....

....

....

....

Stick a photograph of your pet here!

Sweet dream diary

When Ariel lived under the sea, she often dreamed of exploring the human world. What do you dream about? Write your dreams here so you can remember them later.

Date: ....

Describe the dream: ....

....

....

How did you feel when you woke up?

....

....

What do you think it meant?

....

....

....

....

Date: ....

Describe the dream: ....

....

....

How did you feel when you woke up? ....

....

What do you think it meant? ....

....

Date: ....

Describe the dream: ....

....

....

How did you feel when you woke up? ....

....

What do you think it meant? ....

....

Magical music

Ariel loves to listen and dance while the underwater orchestra plays its instruments. What music do you like?

Who is your favorite singer or group? ....

....

Which song always makes you want to dance?

....

....

Which instrument can you play? If none, which one would you like to play? ....

....

....

What would you call your group?

....

....

Use this page to write some words that could be turned into a song. Try to use rhyming words like "fish" and "wish".

Perfect plans

Every princess has dreams and wishes for the future. What are yours? Try to imagine yourself in ten years' time.

How old will you be?

....

Where will you be living?

....

What will you do each day?

....

....

....

....

Where will you go on vacation?

....

Who will be your best friend, and why?

....

....

....

....

....

....

Who will you live with?

....

....

Draw a picture of what you think you'll look like in the future.

January

My favorite thing about January:

....

....

....

The best thing
I did this month:

....

....

....

....

....

....

....

In January, the weather was:

....

Birthdays that
were in January:

....

....

....

....

....

....

....

....

Favorite animal
moment this month:

....

....

....

....

February

My favorite thing about February:

....

....

....

The best thing I did this month:

....

....

....

....

....

....

....

In February, the weather was:

....

Birthdays that were in February:

....

....

....

....

....

....

....

....

Favorite thing my best friend did this month:

....

....

....

....

March

My favorite thing about March:

....

....

....

The best thing
I did this month:

....

....

....

....

....

....

....

In March, the weather was:

....

Birthdays that
were in March:

....

....

....

....

....

....

....

....

The best dream
I had in March:

....

....

....

....

April

My favorite thing about April:

....

....

....

The best thing
I did this month:

....

....

....

....

....

....

....

In April, the weather was:

....

Birthdays that
were in April:

....

....

....

....

....

....

....

....

Something new
I learned in April:

....

....

....

....

May

My favorite thing about May:

....

....

....

The best thing
I did this month:

....

....

....

....

....

....

....

In May, the weather was:

....

Birthdays that
were in May:

....

....

....

....

....

....

....

....

A secret wish
I made in May:

....

....

....

....

June

My favorite thing about June:

....

....

....

The best thing
I did this month:

....

....

....

....

....

....

....

In June, the weather was:

....

Birthdays that
were in June:

....

....

....

....

....

....

....

....

A new treasure
I found in June:

....

....

....

....

July

My favorite thing about July:

Birthdays that were in July:

The best thing I did this month:

A new friend I made in July:

In July, the weather was:

August

My favorite thing about August:

....

....

....

The best thing
I did this month:

....

....

....

....

....

....

....

In August, the weather was:

....

Birthdays that
were in August:

....

....

....

....

....

....

....

....

A new favorite
place I found:

....

....

....

....

September

My favorite thing about September:

....

....

....

The best thing I did this month:

....

....

....

....

....

....

....

In September, the weather was:

....

Birthdays that were in September:

....

....

....

....

....

....

....

....

The best place I visited:

....

....

....

....

October

My favorite thing
about October:

....

....

....

The best thing
I did this month:

....

....

....

....

....

....

....

In October, the weather was:

....

Birthdays that
were in October:

....

....

....

....

....

....

....

....

A new dream I
have for the future:

....

....

....

....

November

My favorite thing
about November:

....

....

....

The best thing
I did this month:

....

....

....

....

....

....

....

In November, the weather was:

....

Birthdays that
were in November:

....

....

....

....

....

....

....

....

My favorite
family moment:

....

....

....

....

December

My favorite thing
about December:

....

....

....

Birthdays that
were in December:

....

....

....

....

....

....

....

....

The best thing
I did this month:

....

....

....

....

....

....

....

My wish for
the new year:

....

....

....

....

In December, the weather was:

....

Things to do

Ariel has found her true love, Prince Eric, and is happy living on land with the humans. But she still has things she wants to learn and do in the future. What is on your to-do list?

To do: ....

....

Target date: ....

To do: ....

....

Target date: ....

To do: ....

....

Target date: ....

To do: ....

....

Target date: ....

To do: ....

....

Target date: ....

To do: ....

....

Target date: ....

To do: ....

....

Target date: ....

To do: ....

....

Target date: ....